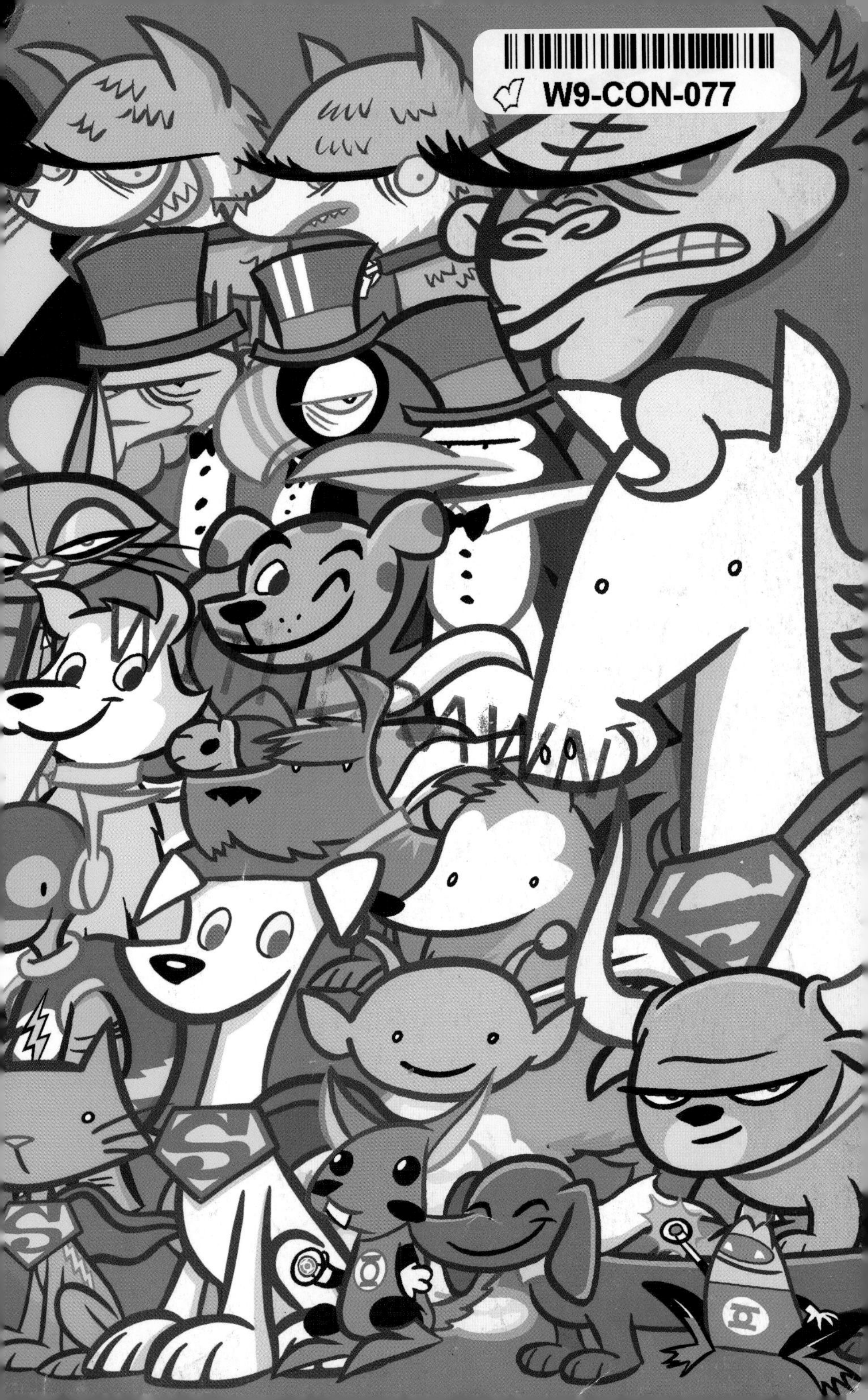

DC SUPER-PETS!™

DC SUPER-PETS!™

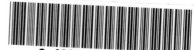

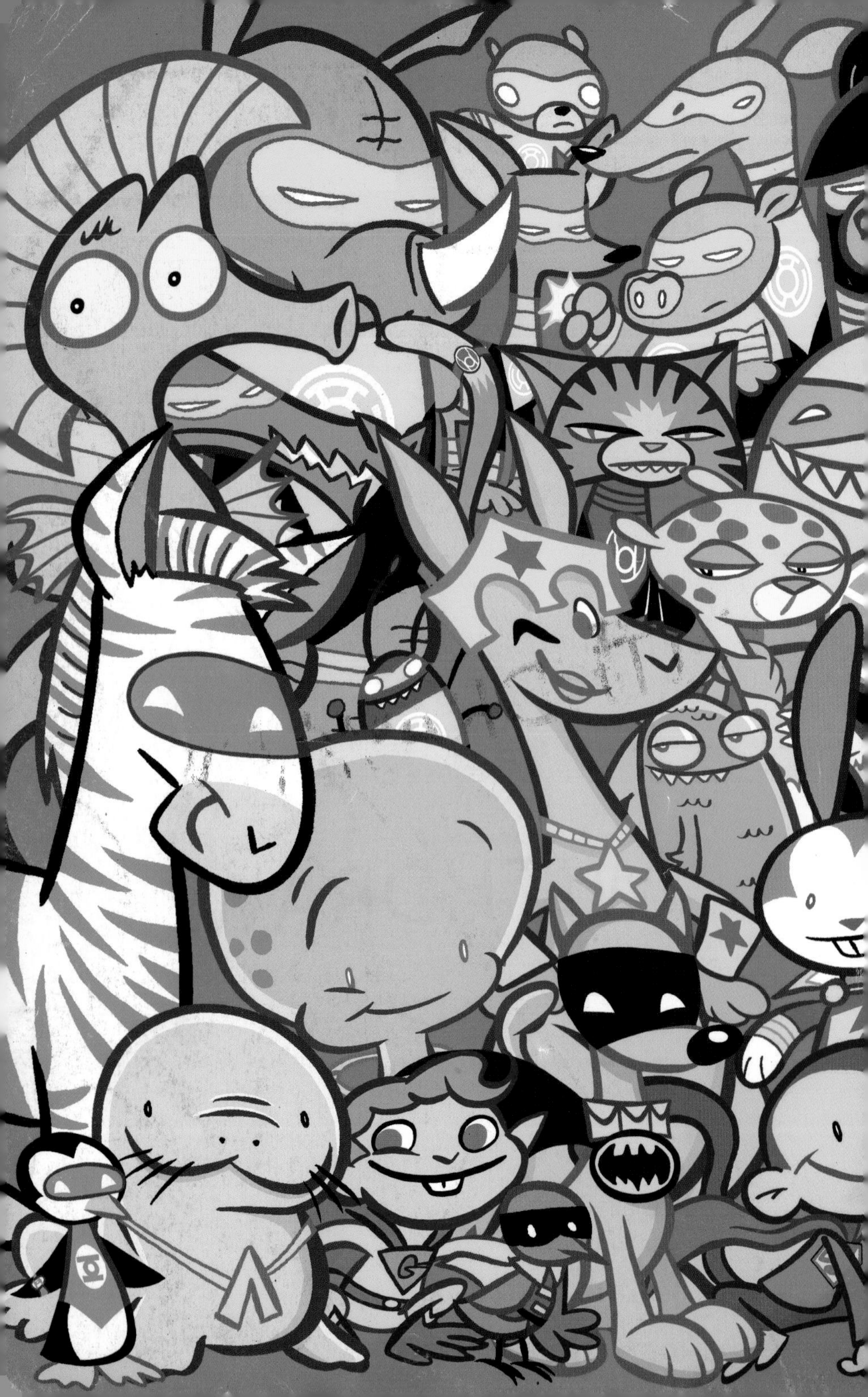

by Sarah Hines Stephens

MIDWAY MONKEY MADNESS

illustrated by
Art Baltazar

Superman created by
Jerry Siegel and Joe Shuster

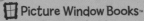

PICTURE WINDOW BOOKS™
a capstone imprint

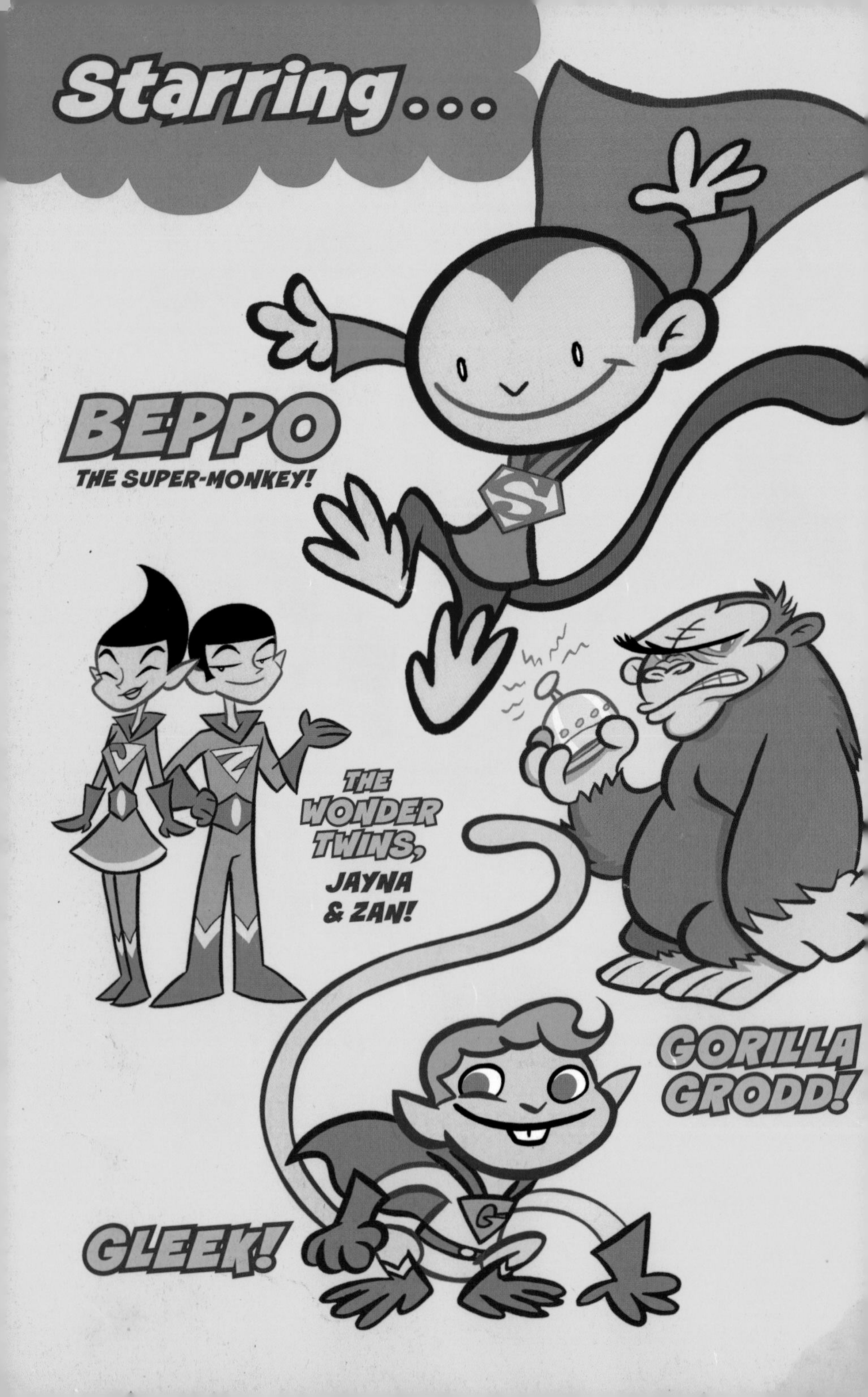
Starring...
BEPPO
THE SUPER-MONKEY!
THE WONDER TWINS, JAYNA & ZAN!
GORILLA GRODD!
GLEEK!

TABLE OF CONTENTS!

FORTRESS OF SOLITUDE
SUPER-COMPUTER

SUPER-PET HERO FILE 003:

BEPPO

Heat Vision

X-ray Vision

Super-hearing

Super-strong
Tail

Super-
breath

Flight

S-shield

4

Super Hero Owner:
SUPERMAN

Species: Super-Monkey

Place of birth: Krypton

Age: Unknown

Favorite Food:
Chocolate-covered bananas

Bio: Moments before Krypton exploded, Superman escaped aboard a tiny rocket ship. He wasn't alone! Beppo hitched a ride as well. On Earth, the Super-Monkey has the same powers as the Man of Steel.

Chapter 1

THE SHOW STOPPER

"**Look! Up in the sky!**" said a kid entering the midway of Bazooka's Carnival. He pointed into the air.

The child hadn't seen a bird or a plane. It was **Beppo the Super-Monkey!** He was on the Ferris wheel. He was enjoying a chocolate-covered banana.

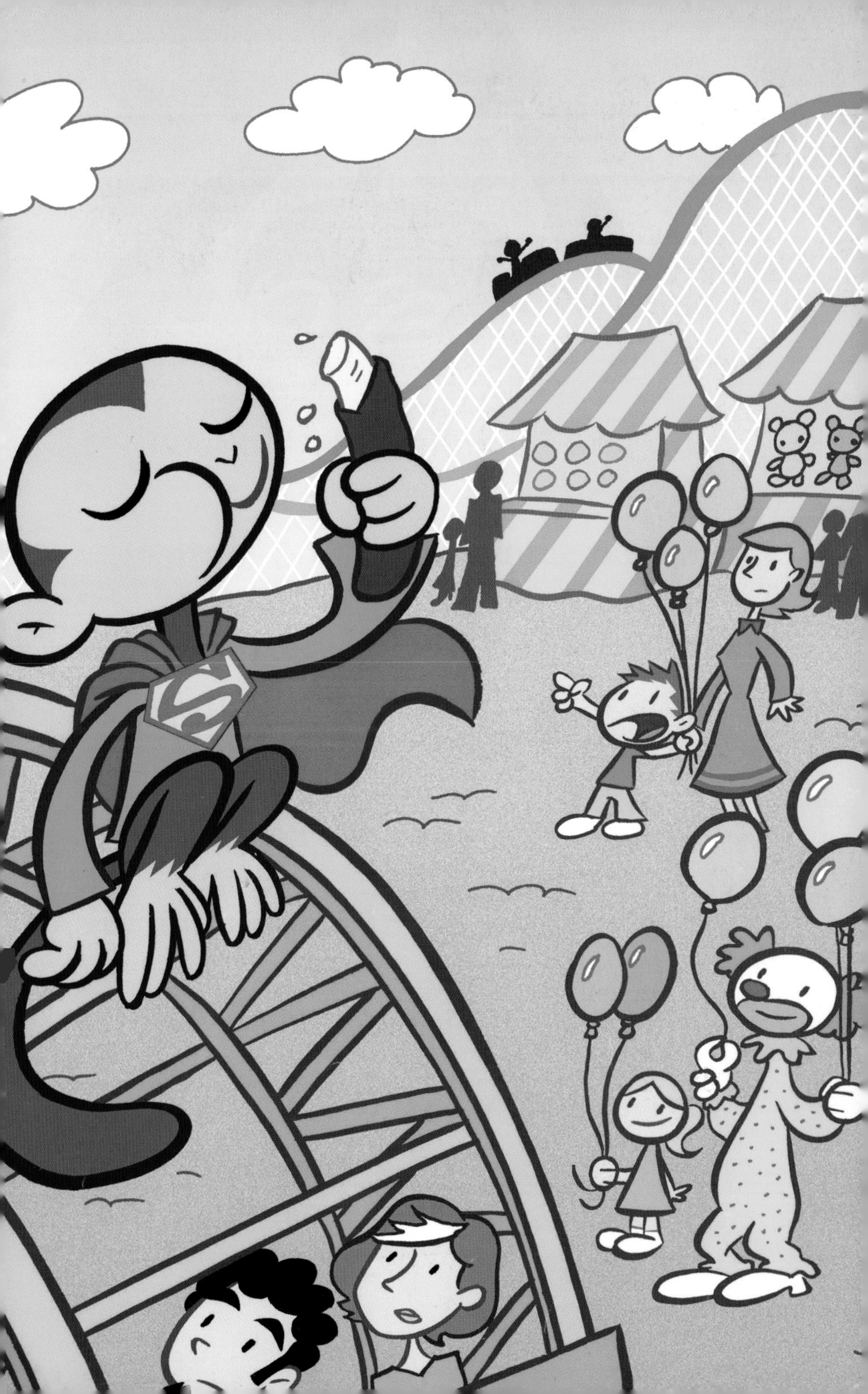

A crowd stood below the animal. Everyone wanted a closer look at the monkey in the cape. They wanted to know how he had climbed so high!

Beppo didn't understand the fuss. But he didn't mind the attention, either. He was having too much fun.

From the Ferris wheel, Beppo could see all of the carnival. He saw animals, rides, and games. The Super-Monkey was choosing which to enjoy first.

Suddenly, he heard screaming!

WOOOOSH!

In a flash, Beppo flew toward the cries. The noises were coming from the animal sideshow. The Super-Monkey flew closer. Terrible growls, yells, and howls joined the screams.

Beppo didn't need super-vision to spot the trouble. The problem was huge! The evil ape, **Gorilla Grodd**, was ripping apart animal cages. He was freeing the wild beasts!

"Be free!" Grodd shouted.

Crocodiles, bears, and zebras were running through the crowd. It looked like the lion was next!

Beppo shook his head. The big cat looked almost as frightened as the crowd of people.

Beppo didn't like to see animals in cages. But setting wild animals loose in a city was a recipe for trouble. It put everyone in danger, including the animals.

Beppo knew Grodd. The gorilla would rather fight humans than free animals. Swinging into action, Beppo shouted at Grodd to stop his monkey business.

Grodd froze. Then he slowly turned. He looked at the little monkey. His eyes became red. The evil ape spotted the large "S" on Beppo's uniform. It was just like the one his enemy, Superman, wore on his chest.

Grodd beat his own chest with his fists. BAM! BAM! BAM!

"You think you can stop me,

Super-Pet?!" Grodd shouted.

Beppo the Super-Monkey didn't

mind being called a pet. He was proud

of the S-shield on his uniform. He was

a mighty super hero!

Yes, Beppo thought. *I can stop Grodd.*

I will protect these people.

GROOARR!

With a roar, Grodd pulled another

bar from the lion cage. The crazy cat

leaped out! The crowd hurried to get

away from the wild beast and the

giant ape.

"Help! Save us!" yelled the crowd.

Beppo flew to the front of the mob.

He had to stop the madness. The

people parted around him.

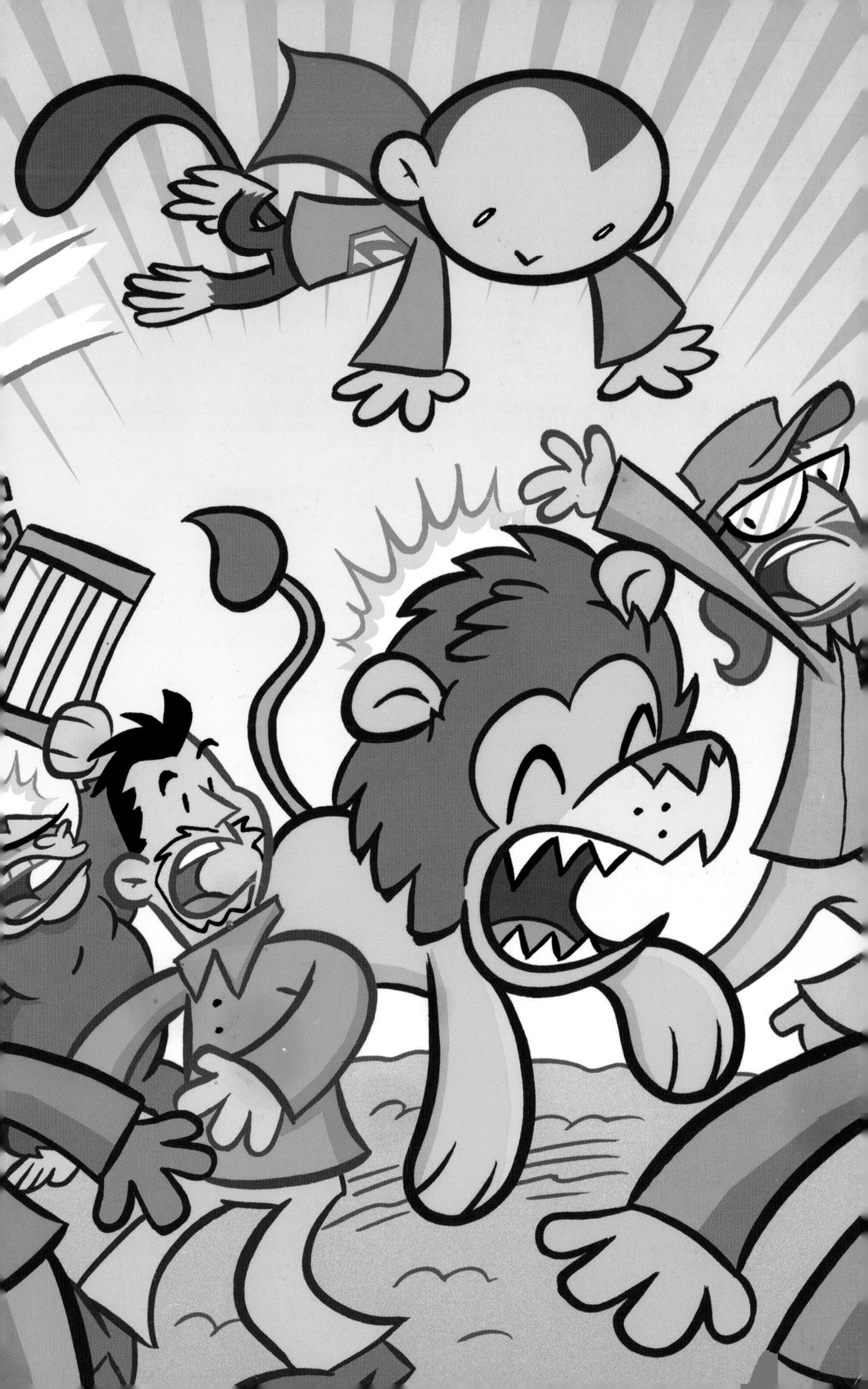

Circus animals and scared people ran in all directions. Beppo needed to sort them out. He had to get the animals away from the people. They needed to go back in their cages.

But how?

Chapter 2

LET THE GAMES BEGIN!

Suddenly, **the Wonder Twins, Zan and Jayna,** appeared beside Beppo. They had come to see the carnival. Like all heroes, they came running when they heard cries for help.

Beppo was happy to see his friends, especially their monkey, **Gleek!**

"Need a hand?" Jayna asked. She

bumped fists with her brother.

"WONDER TWIN POWERS ACTIVATE!"

the twins shouted into the air.

"Form of . . . an ice corral!" Zan said.

"Shape of . . . a sheep dog!" Jayna said in return. The twins transformed.

In their new forms, they started herding the frightened animals into the corral.

Gleek headed for the gate. Beppo called out to the blue monkey. "Let them handle the animals," he said. "We've got bigger problems!" The Super-Monkey pointed toward Grodd.

The super-sized ape was holding a cotton candy machine in the air. He had eaten all of the pink fluff out of it. Grodd was about to toss the metal box into a crowd.

Grodd saw Beppo looking. He threw the machine over his shoulder with a laugh. HAHAHA!

WOOSH!

Beppo flew to the rescue! The Super-Monkey caught the heavy machine before it could hurt anyone.

"Who let you off your leash?" shouted Grodd. Then he saw Gleek. His lip curled in anger. **"You brought a friend? Now there are two of you trained fools?"**

Beppo the Super-Monkey was not about to be teased. He wasn't about to let Grodd catch on to the Wonder Twins' clean-up plan either.

"Strength isn't everything," Beppo told the ape. **"It's time we cut you down to size."**

"Are you challenging me?" Grodd asked. He let out an evil laugh.

HAHAHAHA!

It was a scary sound. But Beppo and Gleek weren't frightened.

"Yes," Beppo said. He looked around and thought fast. **"We're challenging you . . . to a midway monkey duel."**

The Super-Monkey pointed toward the carnival game booths. Gleek's eyebrows shot up with surprise.

"You think you can beat me at some silly human stuff?" Grodd wondered aloud. "The only thing worse than working for humans is playing their simple games. This should be easy!" The gorilla crossed his strong arms.

"But you have to play fair," Beppo said, laying the ground rules. **"No mind games!"**

Grodd had the power to control other people's thoughts. He could move things with his mind. Getting the villain to play fair wouldn't be easy.

"Crushing you will be no problem,"
Grodd said. "Why don't you go first?"

A colorful board of balloons hung
at the back of the first game booth.
Beppo picked up an armful of darts.
He whipped them at the board.

The Super-Monkey popped them all.

Gleek put more balloons up on the board. Beppo stepped back to give Grodd a shot. The gorilla picked up a giant dart. He wound up and threw.

SMAAAASH!

His first dart sailed all the way through the board. It buried itself in the dirt. When the giant darts had all been thrown, three balloons still hung on the board.

"He cheated!!" Grodd shouted. The evil ape believed Gleek had made the game harder to beat.

Gleek shook his head. Beppo quickly soared toward the next game.

The ring toss was one of Beppo's favorite games. He had just the right touch. Every ring he threw circled the top of a milk bottle.

FWIP! FWIP! FWIP!

If they were playing for prizes, he would have earned a stuffed toy as big as Grodd!

On the other hand, the evil ape couldn't even hit the milk bottles. Without his mind powers, he was just an overgrown gorilla!

Gleek snickered.

It was hard enough for Grodd to lose at human games. Being laughed at by a space monkey was the last straw. His eyes turned red. His anger took over.

The giant gorilla smashed the game booths like they were made of cardboard. Milk bottles flew. Prizes spilled onto the grass.

With evil in his eye, Grodd turned on Beppo and Gleek. "I was wrong about you two. You're worse than silly pets in your little outfits," Grodd shouted. **"You're clowns!"**

Using his mind powers, the villain carried Beppo and Gleek through the air. He threw them in a cage.

He locked the metal prison shut with his mind. **SLAM!**

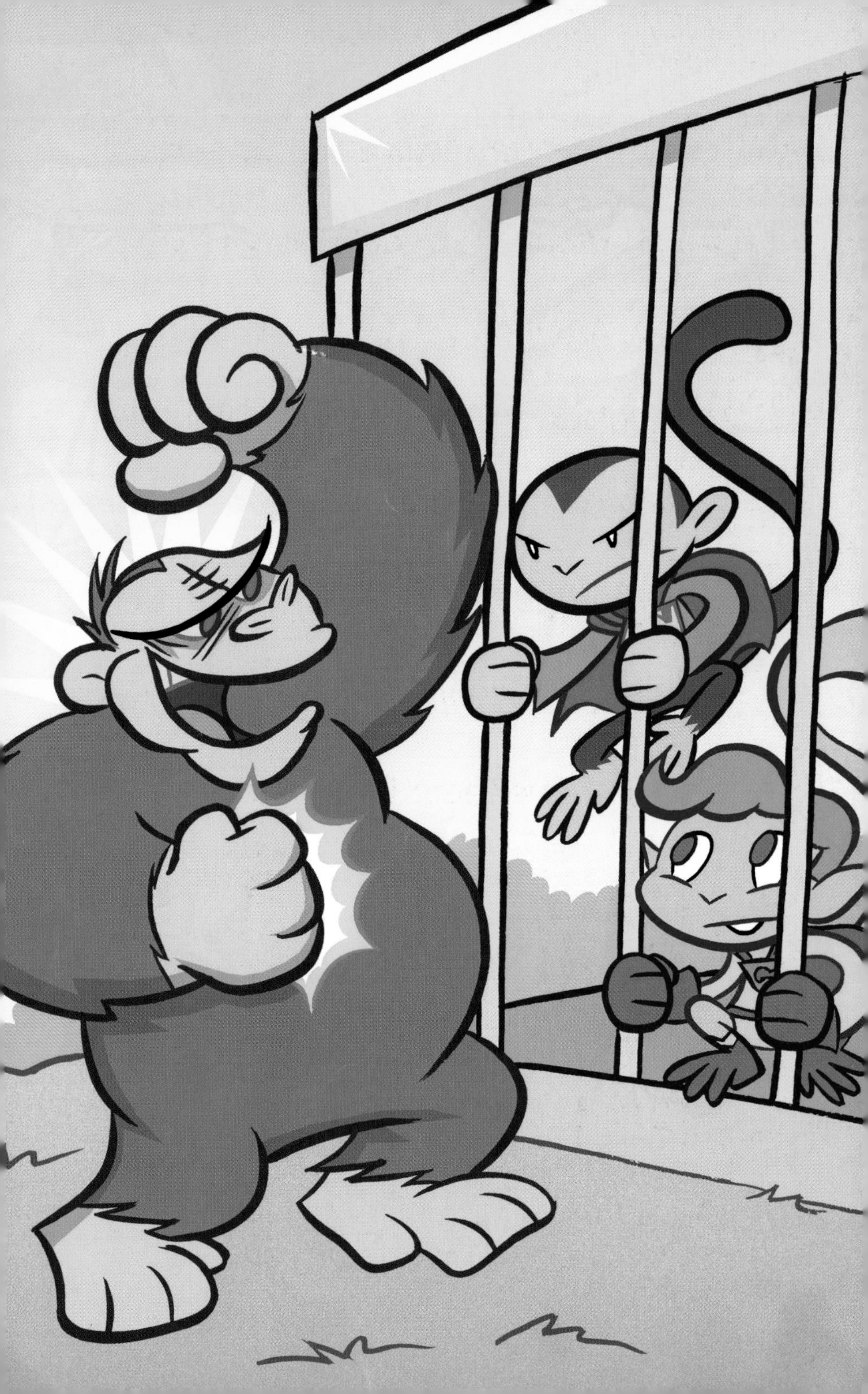

HAHAHAHA!

Grodd laughed at his prisoners.

Gleek screamed in fright. He had been a carnival animal before. Long ago on the planet Exxor, he had performed under the big top. Zan and Jayna had been there, too.

Just the memory of those days made Gleek shiver. The little blue monkey sat in the corner of the cage, helpless.

Chapter 3

BRINGING DOWN THE HOUSE

Luckily, no cage could hold Beppo.
As long as humans and animals
were in danger, nothing could stop
him. Using his heat vision, the Super-
Monkey melted the steel bars.

ZRRRRRT!!!

Pulling Gleek along, Beppo flew after Grodd. The monster had finally seen the Wonder Twins' plan.

All of the circus animals had been rounded up by Jayna in her sheep dog form. The beasts were safely contained in Zan's ice corral.

Outside the fence, people stumbled around in fear. Grodd walked toward them with angry eyes.

The gorilla giant towered high over the helpless crowd. ROAR!!

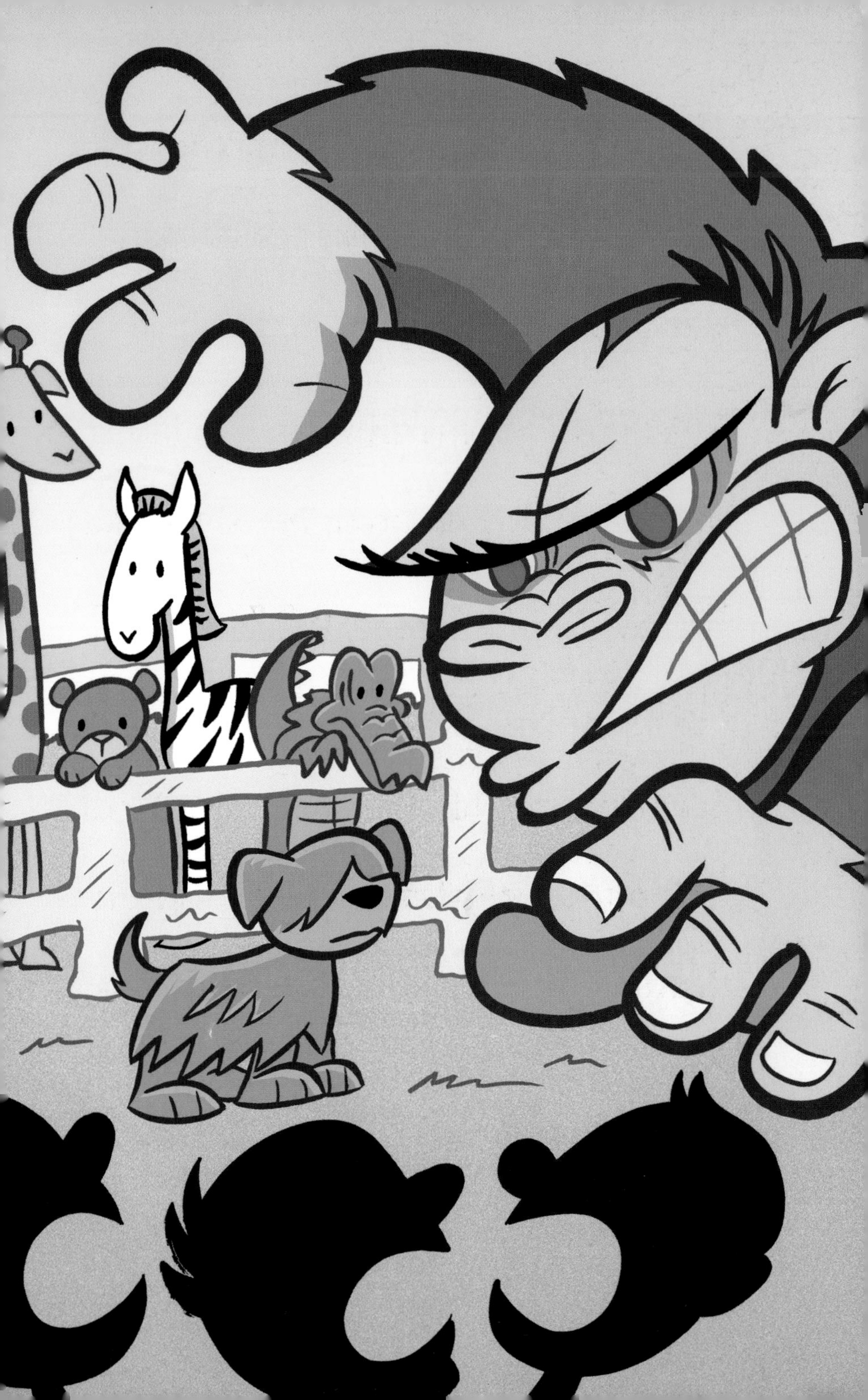

The only things even close to the giant ape's size were the circus elephants. These beasts had helped raise up the huge big top.

That gave Beppo an idea.

Freed from the cage, Gleek was ready to help. The first thing they needed to do was to get Grodd to look at them.

WHHIRRRRRRRL

Gleek's tail began to spin like a helicopter. He lifted off. He headed toward the snack stand.

In a flash, Beppo and Gleek were back and armed. They swooped around Grodd's head. At the same time, they threw corn dogs, snow cones, churros, and chocolate sauce at the angry ape. SPLAT!

The villain swung at them. He missed each time. Gleek and Beppo dodged, dipped, and threw a few corncobs-on-a-stick.

WHAP! SPLAT!!

Covered in food, Grodd opened his mouth to roar. His timing was perfect. At that moment, Beppo launched a gallon of soft serve ice cream at the target. Gleek topped it off with a cherry. Bull's-eye!

SPA-LOOP!!

Before Grodd could move, the
monkeys headed for the big top.

Wiping sticky vanilla goo from
his eyes, Grodd followed. Beppo had
hoped that would happen.

The Super-Monkey flew into the tent with the giant gorilla on his heels. Grabbing the trapeze artists' net, he stretched it across the doorway. Grodd walked right into Beppo's web. The ape got twisted in the net.

Outside, Gleek worked as fast as he could. He loosened the ropes that held up the big top.

In the tent, Beppo loaded the clown's cannon with popcorn. He fired! The popcorn blinded Grodd. He roared and swung his fists in Beppo's direction.

Beppo was ready. He was flying near one of the giant poles that held the tent up. POW! Grodd was powerful, but Beppo was fast. Beppo dodged and Grodd missed again. SMASH! And again.

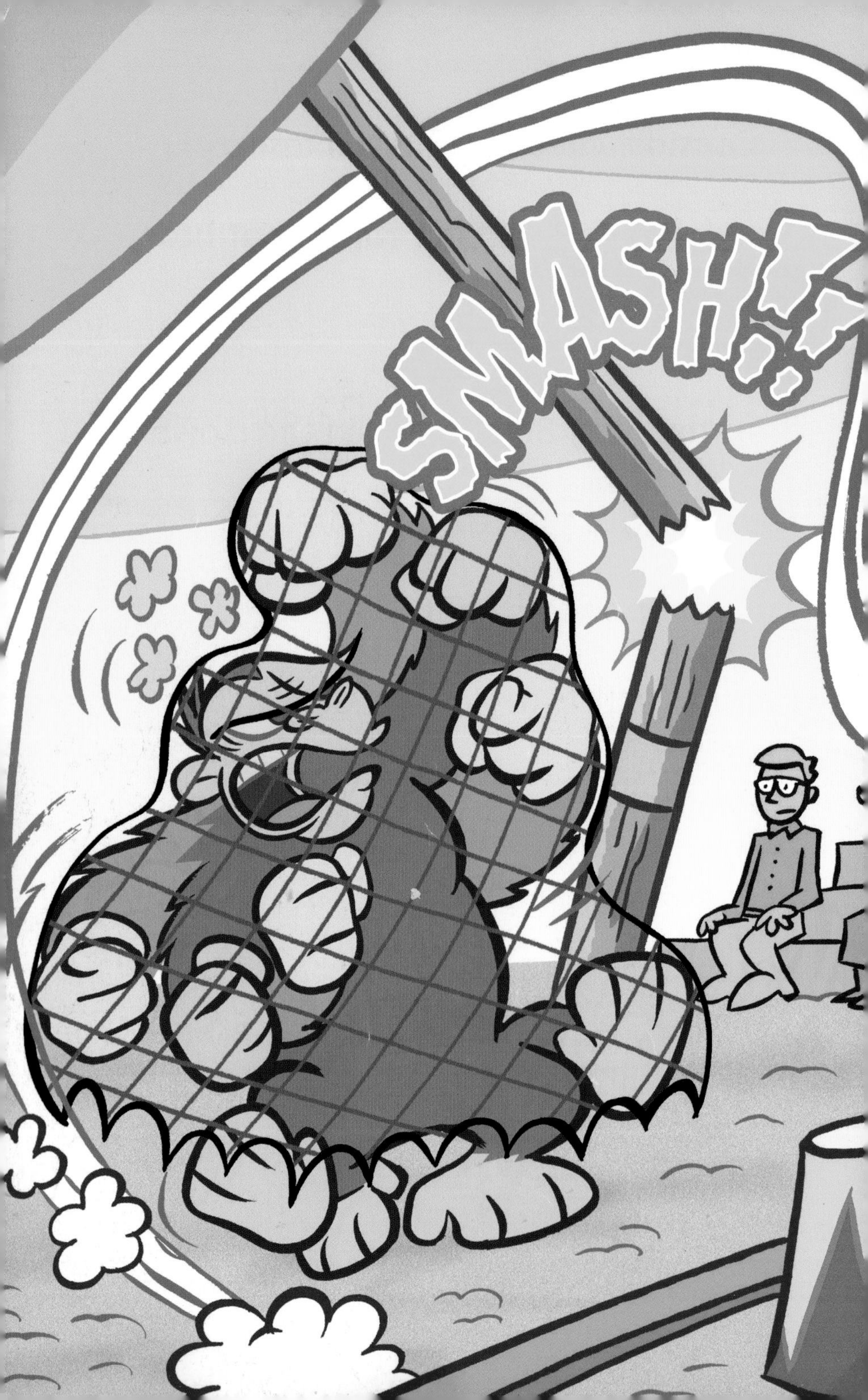
SMASH!!

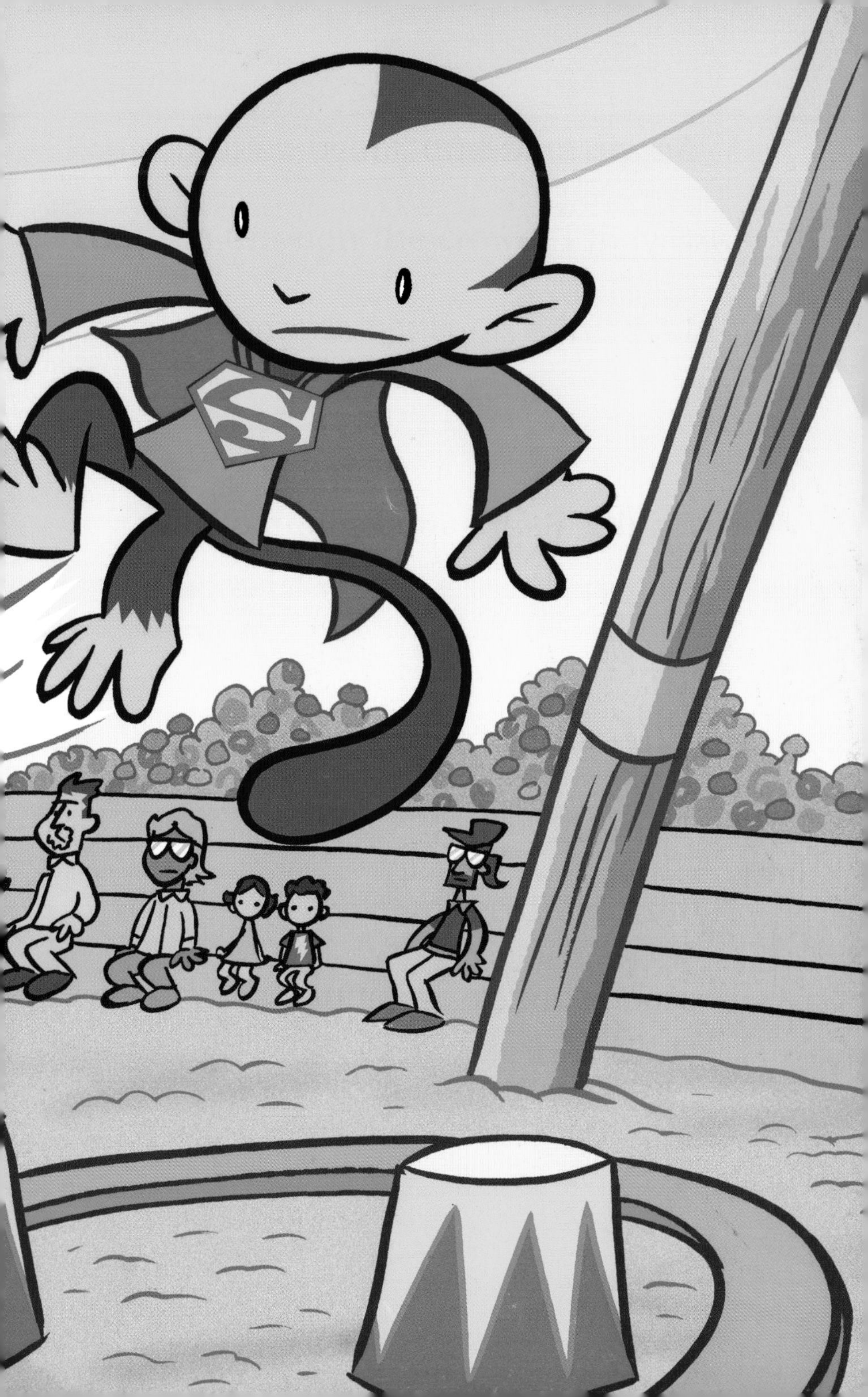

Beppo smiled. Grodd's misses were just what the super hero wanted. Each time the ape smashed another pole, the tent swayed a little more.

Finally, Beppo ducked out of the tent. He took to the sky. *WOOSH!*

The Super-Monkey told Gleek to make sure all the people were standing clear. Jayna helped. She guided everyone toward safety with her barks.

The grunts and roars from inside the tent sent chills down Beppo's spine. His plan was working. The ropes that had held the tent up were ripping loose, thanks to Gleek.

It was time to bring down the house!

Beppo took off. He picked up speed. Faster and faster Beppo flew around the brightly colored tent. He created a tornado of air.

The force of the wind spun around Grodd like a cocoon. It wrapped him tight in the heavy tent.

The crowd cheered. The strongman lifted Gleek and Beppo onto his shoulders. The elephants trumpeted loudly to their heroes.

Even the ringmaster came over to
thank Beppo and Gleek. "The show
must go on," he said.

"Hip, hip, hooray!" the crowd
shouted together.

Beppo loved the carnival. It was his favorite place! But now, the carnival was even better since he could enjoy it with his friends.

And Grodd — the midway's Big Top Banana — was a sideshow smash!

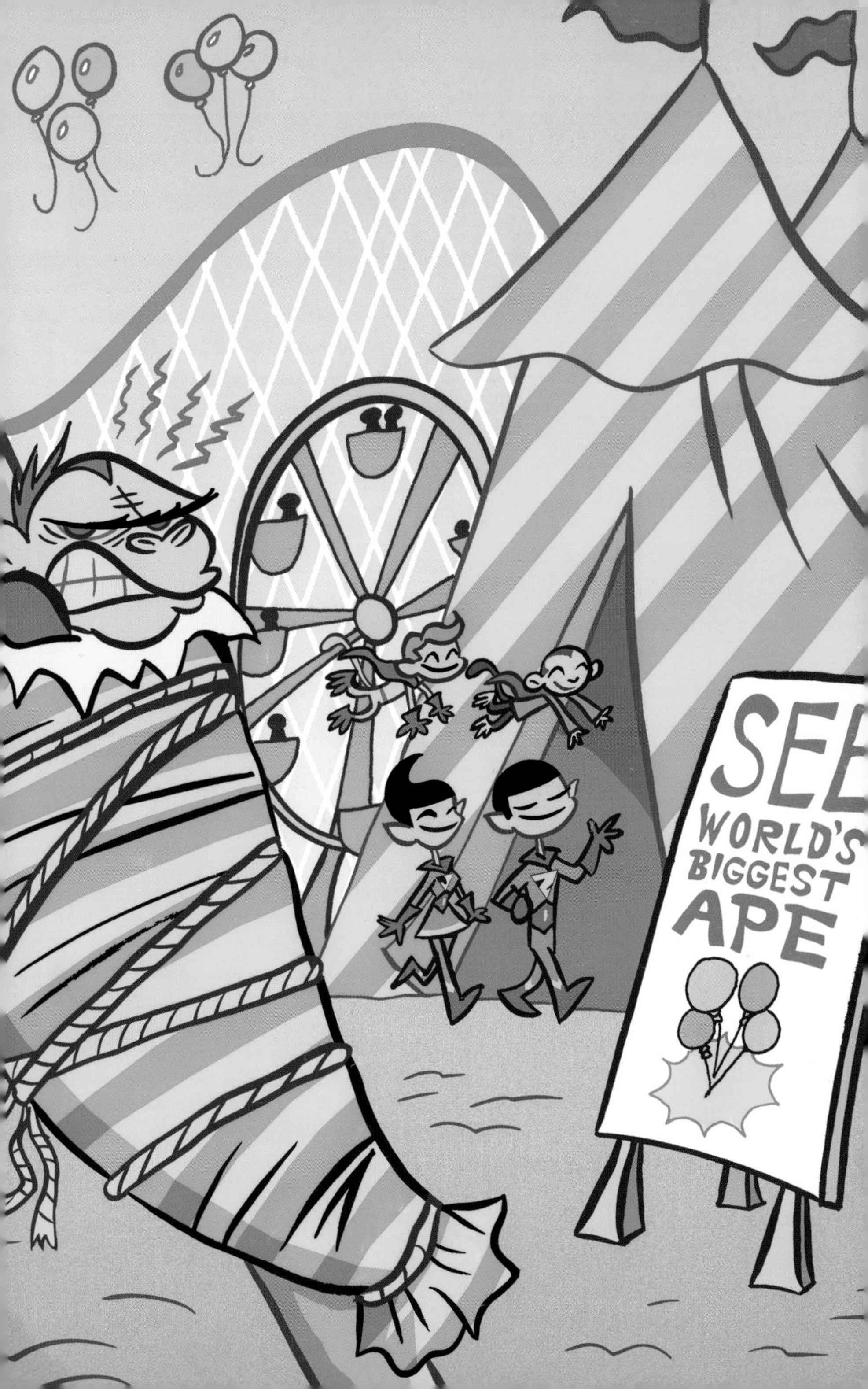
SEE
WORLD'S
BIGGEST
APE

KNOW YOUR

Krypto

Streaky

Beppo

Comet

Ace

Jumpa

Whatzit

B'dg

Storm

Topo

Ark

Hoppy

Paw Pooch

Bull Dog

Chameleon Collie

Hot Dog

Aw yeah, **HERO PETS!**

Tail Terrier

Tusky Husky

SUPER-PETS!

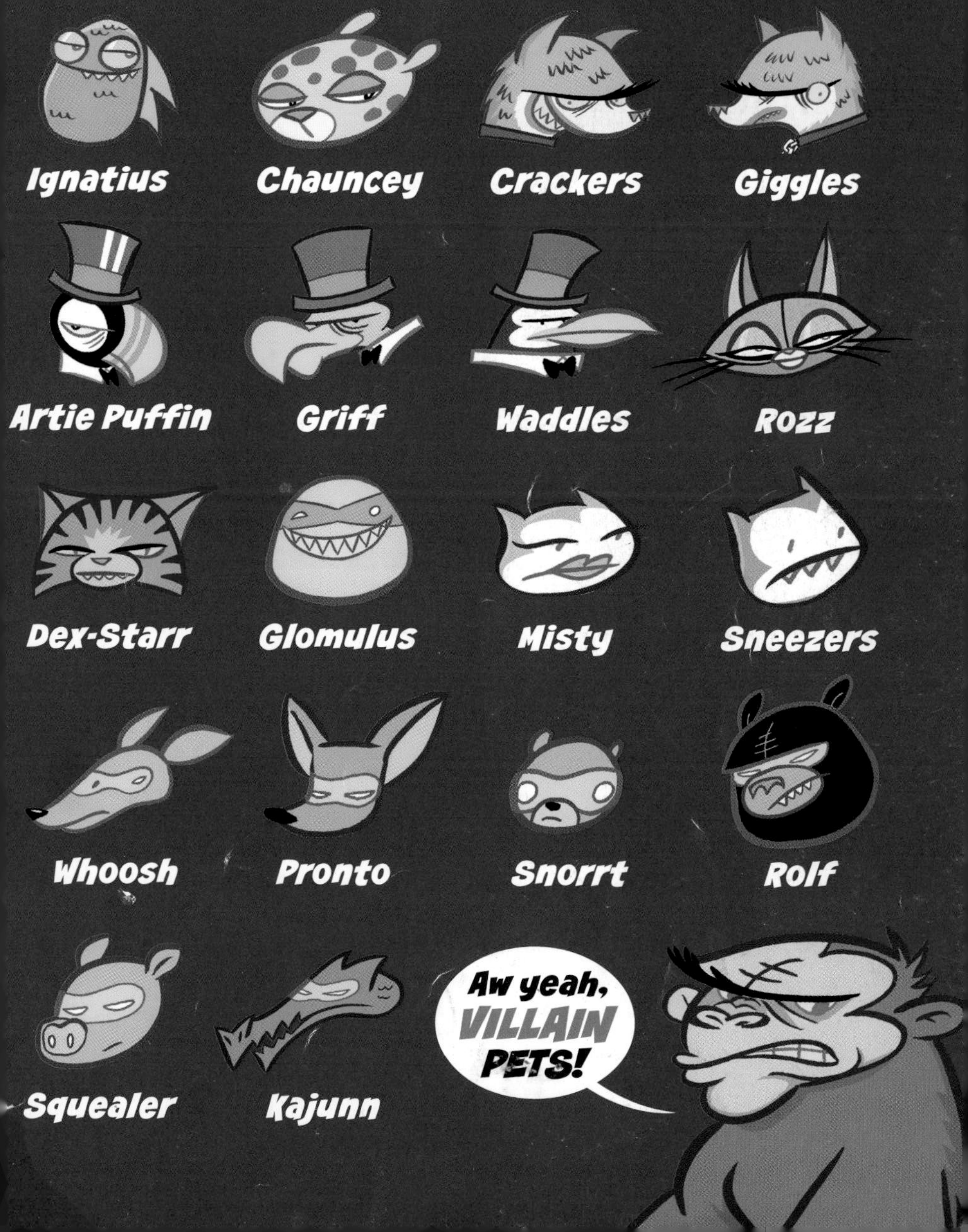
Ignatius
Chauncey
Crackers
Giggles
Artie Puffin
Griff
Waddles
Rozz
Dex-Starr
Glomulus
Misty
Sneezers
Whoosh
Pronto
Snorrt
Rolf
Squealer
Kajunn
Aw yeah, VILLAIN PETS!

AW YEAH, JOKES!

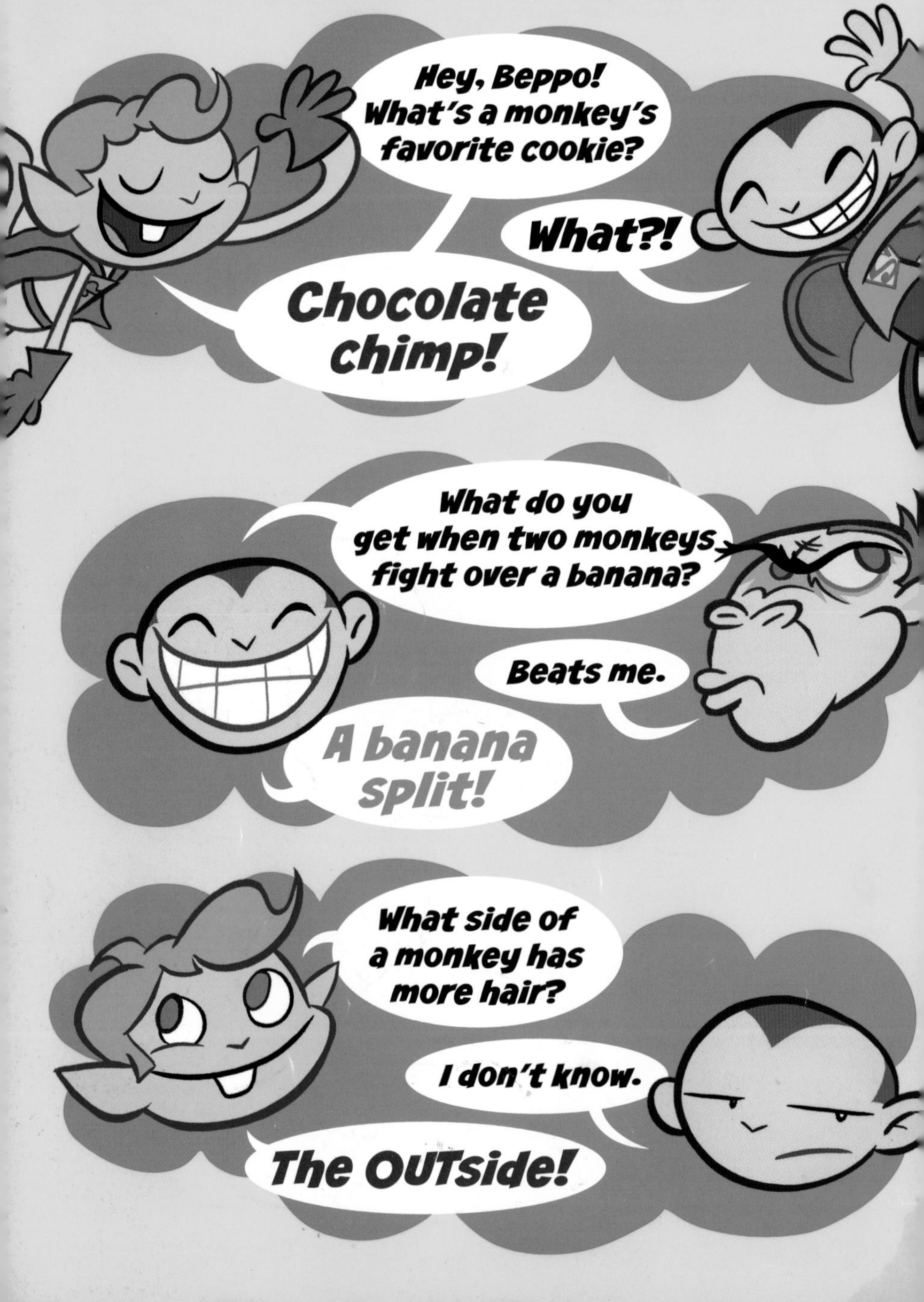
Hey, Beppo! What's a monkey's favorite cookie?
What?!
Chocolate chimp!
What do you get when two monkeys fight over a banana?
Beats me.
A banana split!
What side of a monkey has more hair?
I don't know.
The OUTside!

WORD POWER!

activate (AK-tuh-vate)—to turn on or cause to work

big top (BIG TOP)—the main tent at a circus or carnival, where performances are held

corral (kuh-RAL)—a fenced area that holds animals

ringmaster (RING-mass-tur)—the person in charge of performances at a circus or carnival

sideshow (SIDE-shoh)—a small show in addition to the main attraction at a circus, carnival, or fair

trapeze (tra-PEEZ)—a bar hanging from two ropes, which circus performers use to swing through the air

uniform (YOO-nuh-form)—a special set of clothes worn by a specific group, such as super heroes

Word Powers...
ACTIVATE!

MEET THE AUTHOR!

Sarah Hines Stephens

Sarah Hines Stephens has authored more than 60 books for children and written about all kinds of characters, from Jedi to princesses. When she is not writing, gardening, or saving the world by teaching about recycling, Sarah enjoys spending time with her heroic husband, two kids, and super friends.

MEET THE ILLUSTRATOR!

Eisner Award-winner Art Baltazar

Art Baltazar is a cartoonist machine from the heart of Chicago! He defines cartoons and comics not only as an art style, but as a way of life. Currently, Art is the creative force behind *The New York Times* best-selling, Eisner Award-winning, DC Comics series *Tiny Titans* and the co-writer for *Billy Batson and the Magic of SHAZAM!* Art is living the dream! He draws comics and never has to leave the house. He lives with his lovely wife, Rose, big boy Sonny, little boy Gordon, and little girl Audrey. Right on!

READ THEM ALL!

DC SUPER-PETS!

THE FUN DOESN'T STOP HERE!

Discover more:

- Videos & Contests!
- Games & Puzzles!
- Heroes & Villains!
- Authors & Illustrators!

@ www.capstonekids.com

Find cool websites and more books like this one
at www.facthound.com Just type in Book I.D.

9781404863057 and you're ready to go!

Picture Window Books™

Published in 2011
A Capstone Imprint
1710 Roe Crest Drive
North Mankato, Minnesota 56003
www.capstonepub.com

Copyright © 2013 DC Comics.
All related characters and elements are trademarks
of and © DC Comics.
(s13)

STAR13048

Cataloging-in-Publication Data is available
at the Library of Congress website.
ISBN: 978-1-4048-6305-7 (library binding)
ISBN: 978-1-4048-6619-5 (paperback)

Summary: When a carnival comes to
Metropolis, the evil ape Gorilla Grodd turns
a festival of fun into a day of destruction!
Beppo the Super-Monkey, along with the
Wonder Twins and their space chimp, Gleek,
must stop his midway madness.

Art Director & Designer: Bob Lentz
Editor: Donald Lemke
Creative Director: Heather Kindseth
Editorial Director: Michael Dahl

Printed in the United States of America
in North Mankato, Minnesota.
032017   010318R

DC SUPER-PETS!™

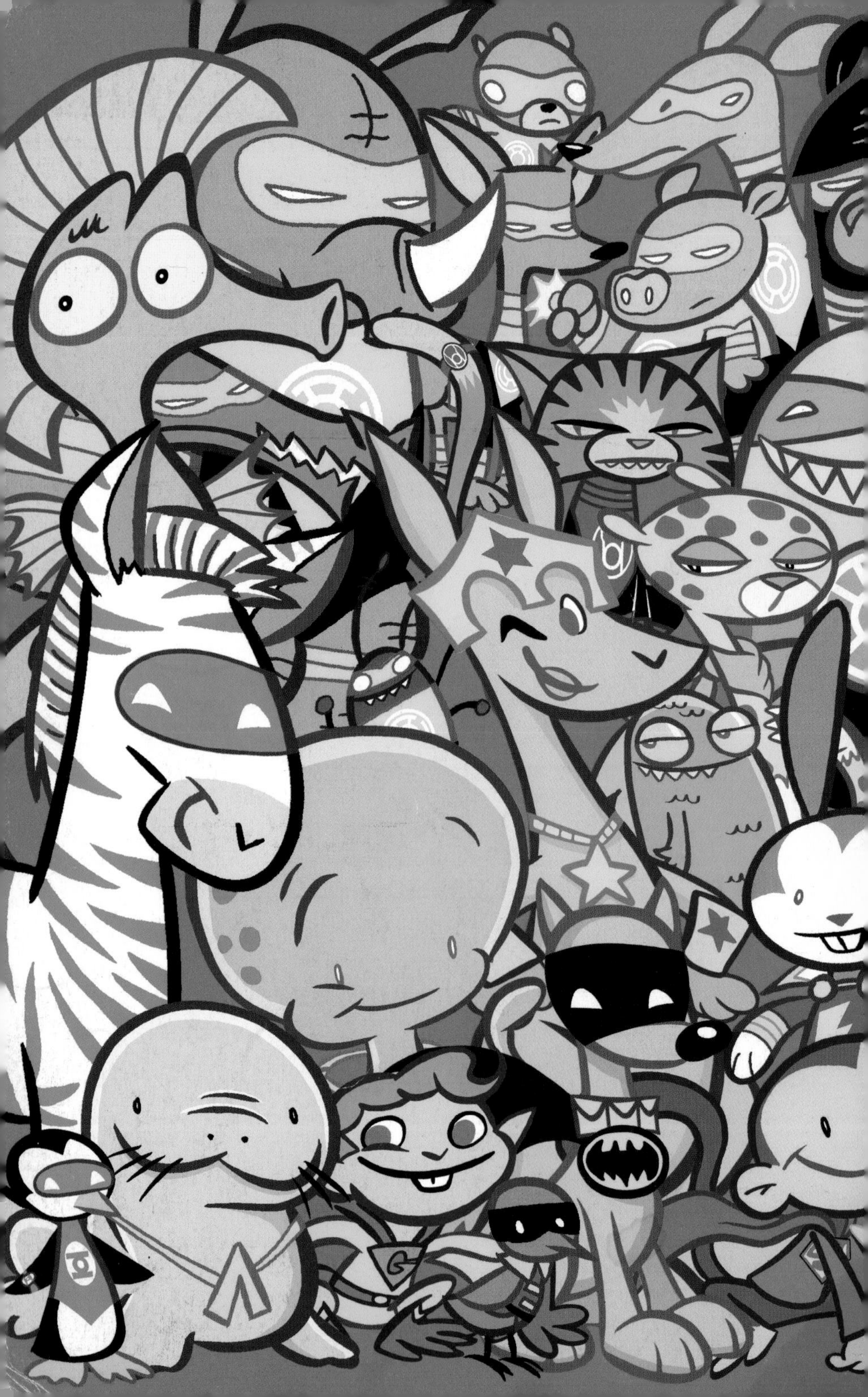

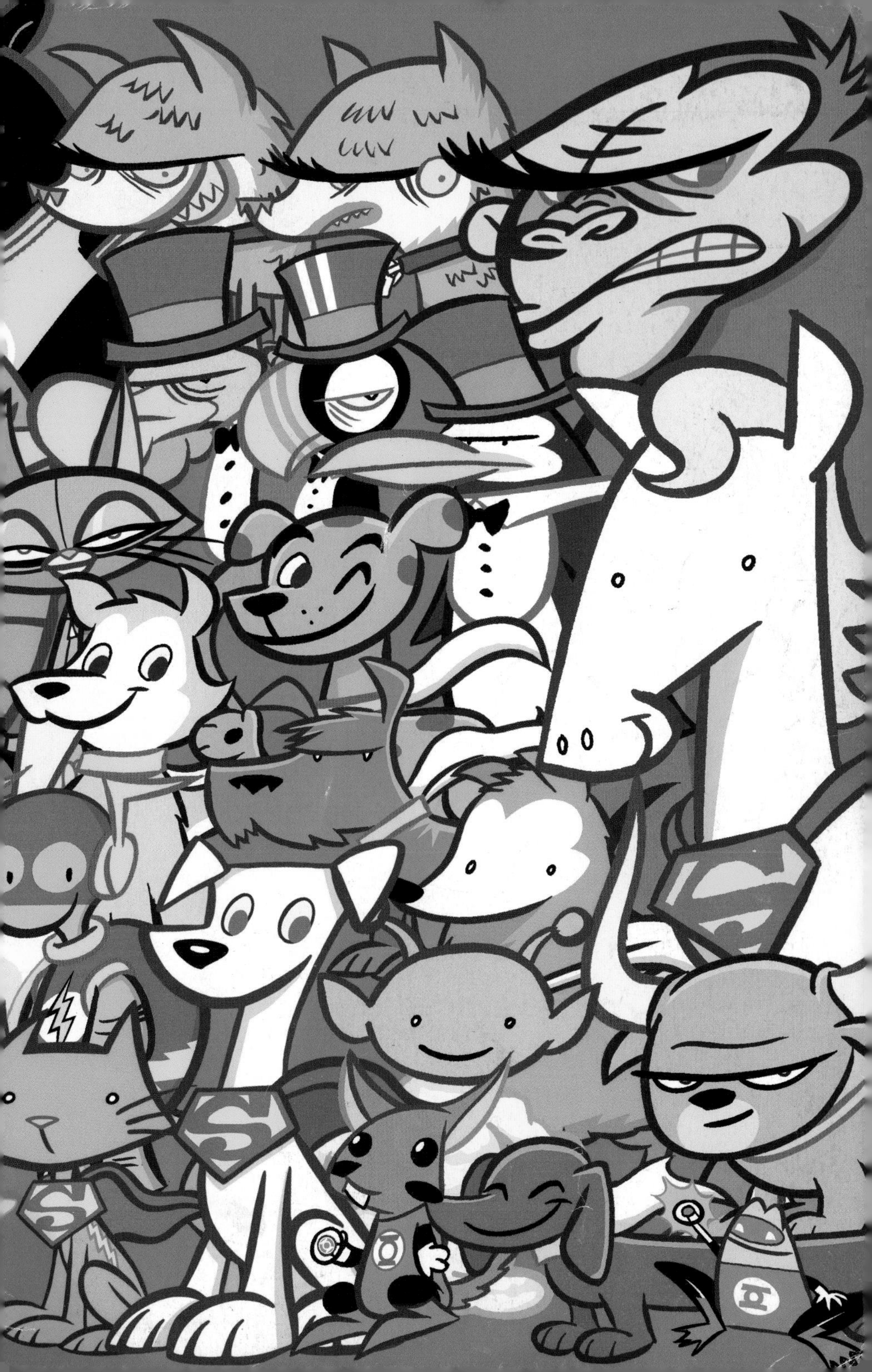

DC SUPER-PETS!™

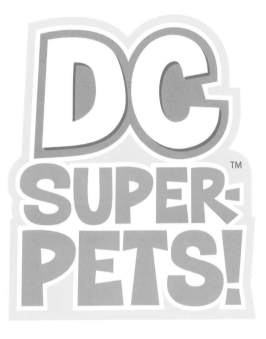